SMART ALEC ALEX

BRACES *AND* GLASSES
IMAGINE THAT!

Copyright © 2020 by Taunya D. Said

First edition 2020

Illustrations by FX AND COLOR STUDIO
www.fxandcolorstudio.com
Book design by Tobi Carter
Edited by Debbie Manber Kupfer

ISBN 978-0-578-65770-7 (paperback)

SMART ALEC ALEX

BRACES *AND* GLASSES
IMAGINE THAT!

By T. D. Said

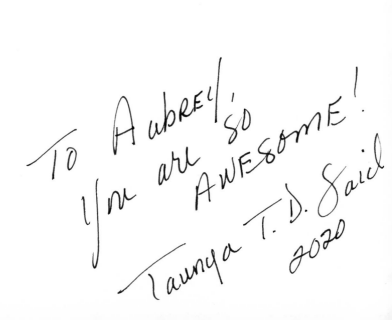

To Aubrey!
You are so
AWESOME!
Taunya T. D. Said
2020

This book is dedicated to my daughter,
India E. Said

Thank you for supporting my dreams. You have
helped me to see all things are possible if you believe.
I appreciate your non-judgmental heart, free spirit
and your positive outlook on any situation.

Thank you for continuing to fill my life with fun
and laughter! You will always be my
PR Professional.

CONTENTS

HEY THERE DUDES AND DUDETTES
ENJOY!

CHAPTER ONE

SAY IT AIN'T SO, PART 1

Hi ya dudes and dudettes, it's me, Alexandria P. Knowitall. I hope you're doing great! I just received some interesting news. My mom said I MIGHT need to get braces, imagine that! I not sure I'm okay with getting braces. I hear kids say all the time they look like train tracks in your mouth.

Hey! But you know me, I investigate why things happen, that's why I'm a Ms. Know-it-all, haha.

There are several reasons why our teeth stick out, like the shape or size of our jaw or if we sucked our thumb or pacifier or even from tooth loss.

I guess I fall into one of these thingies. When I was a little girl, I use to suck my thumb. It was the only thing that made me feel secure. You know… like a blanket.

My mom allowed me to suck my thumb whenever I cried when I was a baby, and it caused my teeth to stick out a little. But I don't care. I think I look just fine."

{{YAWN}}

It's Friday night and I plan to watch a movie, but I'm getting so sleepy.

{{YAWN}}

Mom… talking… about… all… this… braces *{{YAWN}}* stuff… has… gotten… me… to… thinking.

I'll….talk….to….you….dudes and dudettes…. later.

Goodnight.

Tossing and turning in my sleep, I hear my mom's voice in the distance.

"Alex dear, let's go!"

"Okay, Mom, I'm coming. What about breakfast?" I yell.

"Dear, we don't have time for breakfast. We'll grab some fast food for lunch, if you behave yourself, Miss Missy," says Mom.

Today Mom is taking me to the dentist to have my teeth checked and cleaned.

She says it looks like I have an overbite. What is an overbite?

I chew my food like smart kids, I don't overbite my food!

Ugh! Why me? Hmm, why not me?

Boy! I really don't feel like myself today. I feel a little strange for some reason. But hey, on with my day.

It may not be so bad wearing braces to the coolest middle school in Georgia—T.K. Spittle. I always keep it positive – I'm a trendsetter!

I can't help wondering what my friends are going to say when they see me. I hope no one teases me; that would be the worst, ha! I wouldn't tease another kid if they had to wear braces—at least not on purpose. I can't help it if I have so many snappy come backs. Hahaha.

Boy! If I need to wear braces, I wonder if I'll be

starting a new thing, everybody likes to follow me, I guess. These things are going to start a new vibe, not everybody likes them, but in some cases it's necessary. I'm not sure I want to be that different. Mom is telling me it's for my own good. Funny, most kids wouldn't see it that way, but my mom is so cool, I get it.

"Mom, are they going to hurt?"

"Is what going to hurt, Alex"? asks Mom.

"The braces."

"Oh Alex dear, no need to worry your pretty little head. You will be just fine!" Mom claims.

"But Mom, I'm trying to be positive about this whole thing, but in my every other thought, a doubt smacks me upside my head."

"Now, stop it, do you want to walk around with your front teeth sticking out like a walrus?"

"I don't care. I would still look different from my friends and that's okay! I would stand out and be the super star of T.K. Spittle Middle School."

"You will really stand out with all of that bling in your month, superstar!" says Mom.

All the way to the dentist office, we keep hitting pot holes. It's a wonder she still has a car.

I have my seatbelt on, but I'm still bouncing all over the place. I only weigh a buck-o-five.

My mom needs a new car, but she wants to hold onto this old dinosaur until it breaks down. When I grow up, I'm going to buy her a big house and a sports car. I love Mom, she's the greatest.

Mom explains we are going to a medical complex for kids only. It's new! The way she talks about it, it's a medical playground for kids.

On the way to the complex, I look it up on the World Wide Web, www.kidsMedicalComplex.com. Looks like a lot of fun, I think. Wait, is it supposed to be fun? Heck if I know.

"Hmm! We're here already?" The drive wasn't that long. Believe it or not, I'm a little nervous. I wish I was in school. Go figure!

The parking lot is already full and it's only 9:30 in the morning. I haven't had breakfast yet, but Mom has promised me fast food at lunch time, IF I cooperate with the dentist.

You see, when I was five years old—that was the first time I saw a dentist and had my teeth cleaned—it was awful! I remember it was in an old office building decorated with clown wallpaper, a clown rug, and the receptionist dressed like a clown. Even the dentist dressed like a clown. I guess they did that for the kids, but not all of us like clowns. I don't like clowns at all. I was sitting back in my chair after my cleaning when the dental assistant told me to rinse my mouth out. I grabbed the cup of blue mouthwash sitting next to me and put it in my mouth to gargle and nearly choked on the mouthwash. The assistant didn't tell me to go to the sink and wash my mouth out. How was I supposed to know? I was just a little kid.

When I almost choked, my legs flew up in the air and knocked over the tray with all the shiny tools the dentist had used to clean my teeth. It scared me to pieces. It was so loud. The dentist ran back to my room to see what happened. When he saw that I'd knocked over his tools, IT didn't look...I mean, *he* didn't look happy anymore. He looked scary. I felt like a baby without her favorite teddy bear.

I'm supposed to get my teeth cleaned once a year in the fall. I guess that's okay. I'm too smart not to have a fresh clean mouth, haha. I don't want to walk around with breath issues, LOL.

Mom and I walk into a big white and blue office building that looks like a block made of Legos. There are lights across the ceiling that look like vines in the jungle and a doorman who opens the door for us and everything. It's so cool.

Coming into the front door on our right there is a snack station with hamburgers, hot dogs, French fries, cakes, chips, and drinks, like coffee, tea and sodas....all the things I like. It doesn't seem very healthy, but I'll take it. And I guess the coffee is for the grown-ups, yuck!

"Can I have a soda, please?" I ask.

"No ma'am, not until your teeth are cleaned and pearly white, besides it's too early for soda," says Mom.

"I bet if I was sixteen, she would let me have a soda," I mumble.

"Excuse me, did you say something?"

"No ma'am."

As I walk beside Mom, I spot a huge foot in my path, so big we have to walk around it. I pass it and then look back… then up. There is a huge elephant in the middle of the lobby floor.

"Whoa! That thing is really big! It looks like it belongs in the jungle or something," I say.

That giant elephant has gotta be fifty feet tall, but why is it smack dead in the middle of the floor like it's on display in a museum?

"Whoa, wait, there are a lot of big statues of animals all over this building." A regular dinosaur park!

I think it's weird, but everyone is walking around like its normal, so I play along.

This place is like an amusement park. The neutral colors and string lights are cool.

The kids' medical center only specializes in laboratory testing, x-rays, and braces and glasses. Hmm, imagine that!

Wow, I've never seen an amusement park inside a building before.

They only have a few rides, but it's just enough to have fun! I can't wait to get on the giant slides.

This is weird. They even have vending machines all over with dental stuff like the color bands for your braces and vending machines with eye glass frames, all shapes, colors and sizes. Over in the corner is an x-ray machine. The kids think it's fun. They pop in and out of that thing just to take pictures of their insides. I want to try it, haha!

CHAPTER TWO

MEDICAL OFFICE OR NOT?

Mom doesn't know what floor we need to go to, so she walks over to a sign that lists all the doctors in the building to see what floor the dentist is on. I wonder if she knows his name? Mom points at the map to show me the office number and I don't like it.

I turn around and see something else bizarre but familiar. The elevator doors are the same doors I saw in a movie where the little girl was lost in a strange land with flying monkeys and stuff. I loved that movie! I wished I was that little girl in it. "Oh koko, where can we be? This doesn't look like Georgia anymore," I act it out. I want to be an actress one day when I grow up, ha ha.

The elevators are emerald green trimmed in gold. They are oddly shaped, almost like a diamond. The numbers of each floor light up two at a time and look like evil eyes staring down at me. Before my mom presses the button to the elevator, the doors opens like a mouth releasing a puff of green smoke. Inside there is a person that works in the elevator, just pressing the buttons for everyone.

Why? Who does that?

I remember I saw this once in an old movie.

I watch Mom as she extends her hand out to push one of the buttons. The operator motions her to stop and asks,

"What floor, madam?"

"Thirteen, please," says Mom

"No! No, Mom, not that number?" I yell.

"What, Alex? The dentist is on the thirteenth floor," says Mom.

I start to get nervous. The palms of my hands are sweaty and I'm hot! The kids at school all say the number thirteen is a bad number.

I remember I used to listen to the older people in my family tell scary stories about ghost and spirits as we sat around on the family's countryside porch. My grandma, Patsy, she is very pale and scary. She lives near the bayou in Wood Crack, South Carolina, near the swampy slimy gator monster! Yes! That's what I said the swampy slimy gator monster.

{{Ding}}

"Thirteenth floor, watch your step," says the elevator operator.

The doors open, and we step out of the elevator straight into what looks like the entrance to a dentist office.

In fact, the whole thirteenth floor is medical offices. It looks like hundreds of individual offices. We don't know if we should go left or right. We pick a side and take our chances. Which one is the right office?

Mom and I walk down a long hallway. Each door has the name of a dentist or a doctor.

"Alex honey, do you remember what room we are supposed to go to? I only remember the floor," Mom says with a laugh.

"Sure, It's room 1313," I mumble.

A double whammy bad number.

We walk and walk then finally I see a bright yellow door. It's office 1313. The name tag on the door reads, Dr. Oliver C. Giggles.

I start to giggle myself. I open the door to enter the office, and I am blinded by color, lots of color. It was almost like the game "Playland".

The office is very modern and equipped with iPads to check-in virtually…name, address, telephone number, date and co-payment.

"What is a co-payment?" I ask.

"Alex, honey, please take a seat while I check you in," says Mom.

Watch this… "Why would I take a seat?

"Mom, where do you want me to put it?"

"What do you mean, Alex?"

"The chair, you told me to take a seat, so where should I put it?" I joke with Mom.

"Honey-child, please sit down!" Mom laughs.

I love that my mom has a sense of humor like me.

I sit down and my knees are knocking together like shattering teeth (oops, maybe I shouldn't mention teeth).

I hear drilling in the background. It's making me so scared. I close my eyes and cover my month with both hands. If I had another pair of hands, I would use them to cover my ears (See no evil, speak no evil, and hear no evil). At some point I know I will have to open wide for the dentist. I hope I don't repeat what I did when I was five, LOL.

In the waiting room there are loads of activity books, board games, and a game station for the kids to play with, but I sit still waiting to be called.

"I'm not afraid, I'm not afraid, I'm not afraid. I'm not a baby, I can do this," I keep telling myself.

I try to tell myself I will be fine, but in the back of my mind, I'm somewhat shy about it.

{{Slam}}

I hear a door slam and a girl comes out. She is dressed like a doctor's assistant and carries a clipboard, so I guess she must be the dental assistant.

Hmm, maybe I'll be a dental assistant one day when I grow up, haha.

"Alexandria P. Knowitall."

"Yes," I answer reluctantly.

"Please follow me," she instructs.

"Mom, are you coming with me?" I ask.

"No Alex, you are only getting your teeth cleaned right now. I'll come back there when it's time for your braces consultation with Dr. Giggles, if you need them. Run along like a big girl now, you will be fine."

As I follow the dental assistant back to the room, the hallway seems to stretch longer and longer. It looks like the hallway in a fairytale book I read when I was younger. The hall appears to be getting longer AND smaller, but it is all in my mind, or is it? I look sideways.

It looks like my dentist has three individual offices in the back and each door is a different color with dental posters of people smiling from ear to ear, I guess to promote good dental health.

"Cheese! You're on candid camera!" I say.

I am guided into the room with the yellow door and seated in the big red dentist chair. I look around and see several shiny objects that are used in a dental check-up.

"Wow! Look at all this stuff," I say nervously.

I have a flashback to my first dental visit when I was a kid. Remember, the one I explained earlier?

The first person I meet is the dental hygienist (hahy-jee-nist). Her name badge says Sadie. She looks very young to me, like Sadie is fresh out of dental school.

"Hi Alex! You look like you've seen a ghost. There is nothing to be afraid of. I am only going to clean your teeth, sweetheart," says Sadie.

Yeah, well, I'm still a kid who doesn't know what to expect.

"How are you going to do that? Do you know how to do that? How long does it take? Is this going to hurt?" I ask, my questions tumbling one after the other.

"Slow down, slow down. I will only be using these tools to scrape the gunk off your teeth," Sadie explains, showing me a bright shiny object that looks like a small hook.

"I don't have gum on my teeth," I protest.

"No honey, gunk—gunk!" says Sadie.

CHAPTER THREE
CHECK-CLEAN-RINSE

Sadie attaches a bib to my shirt and asks me to lie straight while she tilts the chair back halfway. She turns on a bright light above my head, so she can see my teeth really well.

"Here Alex, put these on," says Sadie.

What is this funny looking thing?

"This is special sunglasses to protect your eyes from the ultra violet rays," says Sadie.

Okay, but they look like space cadet glasses.

And what's that?

"Oh, this little thing, well it's a scaler. I will use this to scrape around your gum line to removed plaque and tartar."

Eww, that sounds gross!

I can't see it yet, but I hear the thing that sounds like a drill in the background. Thank goodness, it's not for me!

I brace myself and close my eyes and Sadie start to scrape one tooth at a time and before I know it, she's done. It didn't hurt at all.

"Now little Miss Knowitall, let's clean your teeth."

You're not done yet?

"No ma'am, we have three parts to finish."

Sadie reaches over me and grabs this silver thingy. It looks like the one thing I am scared of the most…the drill!!

She put some pink gooey stuff on the… Oh, it's an electric toothbrush, silly me, LOL.

The brush on the silver electric handle is spinning out of control. She opens my mouth wide and brushes my teeth with the pink gritty gooey stuff.

I like Sadie. She is very good at making me feel comfortable, but she is not the one I'm worried about.

"All done! See that wasn't so bad, was it?" says Sadie.

"No, I guess not,"

"Good! Now go to the sink and rinse the pink gritty gooey stuff out of your mouth."

"What is this stuff? It doesn't have a great taste."

"The pink gritty gooey stuff is just toothpaste, Alex," Sadie says laughing. "It cleans teeth and protects gums.

Okay, this is the last step, Alex! Pick a flavor, any flavor."

Sadie pulls out four white tubs that say fluoride. On the caps it says grape, bubble gum, strawberry, and cherry.

"Hmm, cherry!"

"Okay, cherry it is. Now before you ask, little Miss Knowitall, this is fluoride and it is going to help fight against cavities."

Sadie takes a plastic mouthpiece and smeared the cherry fluoride in it and placed it into my mouth and instructs me the bite down.

"Alex, wait one minute then go rinse that out."

I walk over to the sink. As I wash my mouth out, the water splashes on the floor. "Whoaaaaa! The floor is slippery." Man, I hold onto the sink, slipping and sliding and trying not to fall. At that moment I don't feel scared. I feel like silly ole me again.

As I'm getting myself together, Sadie, the dental hygienist, packs up all the tools she used to clean my teeth and puts them in a sterilizer to be cleaned for other patients.

Sadie starts to leave the room, but before she does, she looks back at me and says, "follow me, the orthodontist area is on the other side of the office."

I step outside the door onto a moving floor.

"Hey! This wasn't here before."

"Just stand still and enjoy the ride," says Sadie.

In two shakes of a tail feather, the moving floor whips us around to the other side.

"Okay, here we are, Braces Room," says Sadie.

When Sadie opens the door, Mom is already sitting in there waiting.

Whoa, this room is cool. There is a vending machine with all colors of rubber bands, just like the one downstairs in the lobby. I wonder what they're for.

"Alex, sit tight. The Orthodontist will be in to see you shortly."

"Ortho-who?" I say out loud.

Gee, I thought my visit was over! I sit in a swivel chair rolling around the floor and twiddling my thumbs. I wait and wait.

What's taking so long? I can't wait to go back out into the lobby area where all the cool rides and stuff are.

Mom is just quietly reading a book.

I may as well sing my favorite song. "Meee! I gotta be meee! Who else would I be? I gotta be meee!!"

I love this old song. For the life of me, I can't remember where I originally heard it. My mom is always listening to old Broadway tunes. That's probably where.

There's a lot of talking outside the door. I wish the dentist would hurry up.

Suddenly the door swings open and in flies the orthodontist, Dr. Giggles.

This guy is smiling so hard it looks like it hurts, and he has on glasses that are thick like soda bottles.

"Hellllllooooo, Ms. Knowitall, and why are we here today?"

I wrinkle my face as his breath is stinky.

"Hi, Dr. Giggles, I am Alex's mother, Mrs. Knowitall. I am here for her consultation."

"Hi ya Doc! I don't think I need braces. I'll be going now."

"Hold it, Miss Missy," shouts Mom.

"Now, now, Alexandria, braces are good for you. They align and straighten your teeth and help position them correctly. Now, don't you want a pretty smile?" asks Dr. Giggles.

Dr. Giggles tries to assure me that braces are not that bad, but I'm not worried, I'm going to look great with or without them—I am a super star!

I smile wide to show my teeth are clean and pearly white, but my goofy smile doesn't hide why I'm really here, this darn overbite.

"Hiiiiiiiii Mrs. Knowitall, I am pleased to meet you. Sit tight while I examine Alex's teeth. Please let me know if you have questions."

Eww, as Dr. Giggles speaks to my mom, it looks like a puff of black smoke is coming from his mouth, and I wonder how he can be a dentist with such bad breath. My mom even makes a face. Haha.

Dr. Giggles leans my chair back and turns on the bright light above my head and shines it into my mouth. This time no sunglasses. I close my eyes.

Even though I am uncomfortable and a bit nervous, Dr. Giggle's breath almost knocks me out! If I'm having work done, I won't need the gas that puts people to sleep.

"Ahhh, Hmmm, oh—yesss, my, my," says Dr. Giggles. "Alex, my child, you have come to the right place! I am going to fix you right up."

"So are you saying Alex needs braces, Dr. Giggles?' Mom asks.

"Wellll, Mother, I want to do some x-rays and look at her mouth from all angles. One moment, I'll be right back. I'll get that started now," says Dr. Giggles.

Before I know it, Sadie comes back into my room and escorts me down the hall to the x-ray room. There is a different person there, a radiologic technologist. She puts a heavy, gray vest on me and sits me down in a chair and puts a hard plastic square in my mouth and tells me to bite down hard. It is very uncomfortable, but I am a trooper!

The radiologic technologist takes pictures of my mouth from all angles. I feel like a modeling star. I twist all around in my chair. I am like, BAM! BOOM! POW! Heyyyyy, work it girl! Haha. Silly me. I almost forget where I am and why I'm here.

"One second, little lady, while I take these to Dr. Giggles," says the radiologic technologist.

More waiting! This dentist visit is the pits. I'd rather be in the waiting room playing the game station. Oh fiddle faddle!

Sadie comes back and escorts me back to my mom, and we wait until Dr. Giggles enters.

"So, Dr. Giggles, what's the prognosis? Does Alex need braces?" Mom asks.

"Yes, yes, my goodness, yes she does. You see here in her x-ray, my dear, the front teeth are pushing forward causing an overbite." He giggles as he talks.

While Mom and Dr. Giggles talk, I look out the window until I overhear that I need braces. I start to pace the floor.

"Okay, okay…I can handle this, yup, I can handle this, I am Alexandria P. Knowitall. I'm smart and funny and I have lots of friends!" I chant. "No need to complain, this is happening. I got this!

"Oh Alex, don't be so dramatic."

"But Mom, you don't understand," I protest.

"Yes, I do, and I understand this discussion is over," says Mom. "Miss Missy, take yourself to the sitting area and wait for me while I finish my conversation with Dr. Giggles."

"Yes ma'am, I'll just wait in the sitting area."

I guess mom can detect I am not feeling this. I guess I'm okay with it. I don't want to walk around looking like a walrus. I half smile.

"Bye, Dr. Giggles!" I say.

"Good day, Alex," says Dr. Giggles.

"Kids!" says Mom.

"It's quite alright, Mrs. Knowitall, Alex will be fine. It just takes some getting used to, that natural," says Dr. Giggles.

I leave and look sad. I have mixed feeling not knowing what my friends will say. It looks like my lips are dragging the floor.

In the meantime, my mom finishes her conversation with Dr. Giggles and makes an appointment for me to get started with my braces.

As we leave the dentist office and head to the elevator, I notice there is a hole right next to it.

"What's this?" I ask.

"Ah, it's a secret passage for kids only. The slide will take you straight the lobby," says the elevator person.

How cool is that!

"Mom, mom can I go down the slide and meet you in the lobby?"

"Sure, sweet pea, if it will make you feel better. See you soon," says Mom.

Yay!! One, two, three –whee!

The slide is fast and loads of fun. At the end I slide out to the middle of the lobby floor, LOL

That night I stay up thinking about ME wearing braces to school, I try not to worry. I'm just a kid. I don't want to worry about grown-up stuff.

— CHAPTER FOUR —

I SMELL MY DENTIST

The next day when I go to school, I see my crew—Candice, Sissy, and Calvin.

"Hey Alex! Where were you yesterday? I didn't see you in school, dudette," says Sissy.

"My mom made me go to the dentist. She says I may need to wear braces,"

"BRACES, yuck!" They all shout together.

"Well Ms. Knowitall, what did the dentist tell you?" asks Candice.

"Mr. Smelly Breath said I need to get braces, and they are going to start putting them on me this weekend," I say.

"But, but wait, wait Alex, why do you need braces? Why do you need braces? And who is Mr. Smelly Breath?" asks Calvin.

"He is my dentist. His name is actually Dr. Giggles and his breath stinks. Boy, it's so bad, it makes the hairs on your neck stand up."

"Eww, no way," says Candice.

"Any who, he said I have an overbite, and my mom said the same thing earlier, go figure."

"So Alex girl, are you going to be able to handle this?" asks Candice.

"Sure, I'm going to wear my braces with pride. Besides it's for my own good," I reply trying to convince myself.

"Look at you being all grown up. Don't go changing on me, LOL," says Candice.

"Nope, not me. I'll always be that kid even when I grow up. I mean, I am a little disappointed, but what is that going to prove? It is what it is, so braces it is. Haha!"

I just lean against my locker holding my head up high. You never let them see you sweat.

Sissy looks at me smiling wide like a silly cat.

"Don't worry, Alex, we won't look at you any differently. You're our best gal pal."

"And you know I have your back," says Candice.

"I know, I know, but really guys, I'm fine!" I smile. "Girls! So, so mushy, yuck!" mumbles Calvin.

Feeling the bond between me and my three BFFs, we move on with our day. The four of us walk into our homeroom class to take our seats before the bell.

{{{RING}}} … Phew! We made it just in time!

Dang! Everyone has taken all the good seats. Oh well, I guess I'll have to sit in the back with Alexia popping gum in my ear. You think if I scare her it will pop all over her face?

"Good Morning *e'tudiant*! (That is "student" in French). Today I would like y'all to copy all ten of the questions on the board and read pages 15 through 25 in your English book and answer the questions," says Mrs. Pew, the French-Country-English Teacher.

I sit down and prepare to copy the questions from the board when I notice the letters are really small.

"Gosh dang it, the board is too far!" I say.

But really, there's only three rows in the classroom, so it isn't too far, but I am having trouble reading the words.

As I write down the questions, I keep squinting trying to make out the words. I stare at the board so hard the letters start to float. I rub my eyes and I blink a few times to try to clear my vision, but nothing helps.

I'm doing my best, but I'm having a hard time. Everything is so blurred.

"Pssssst, Sissy, are you having trouble seeing the board?" I whisper.

"No Silly-Willy, I see it just fine," says Sissy.

"Pssssst, Calvin, are you having trouble seeing the board?"

"No, no, shhhh, not, not while I am writing," says Calvin.

"Pssssst, Candice, are you having trouble seeing the board?"

"No, I have 20/20 vision, girlie," says Candice.

"Me too," I say, knowing I'm not telling the truth.

I turn around to see what everyone else is doing. I can't find anyone in my class who is having the same issues, so I try to ignore it.

Mrs. Pew sees me squinting and summons me to the front of the classroom. I walk to her desk and stand there like a bump on a log.

"Alex, my little tumbleweed, are you having trouble seeing the blackboard?" says Mrs. Pew.

"No, ma'am, I can see just fine. I can even see the small writing on the bottom of your book. My eyes are perfect!" I say.

All the while I'm looking at the board squinting.

I go back to my seat and sit down hoping Mrs. Pew will stop looking at me and she does.

I'm so relieved. Oh no, It looks like Mrs. Pew is jotting down some notes. She's famous for calling our parents.

I continue to write, but my eyes starts hurting, and eventually I stop writing.

"Alex, what are you doing?" whispers Candice.

"Dudette, I'm just sitting here twiddling my thumbs," I say sarcastically.

"Huh?" says Candice.

"I can't see the blackboard, it's blurry," I whisper.

"Alex, do you need glasses?" whispers Candice.

"No, I do not. My eyes are good. They are just tired" I reply.

"No girl, I think you need glasses," says Candice.

"Alright you two, break it up. There will be no talking. Please finish up before the bell rings," says Mrs. Pew.

I pretended to keep writing, but I am going to have to ask one of my BFFs if I can copy the sentences from one of them. The whole day goes by and in each class, I have the same issue.

On the way home on the bus Candice teases me and keeps telling me I may need glasses.

I shrug. "I rubbed lotion on my face this morning and got some in my eyes. Maybe that's the problem."

"Hey Alex, here you go, copy down the sentences from English class," says Candice.

"Thanks, dudette!"

"I can't believe what's happening, first the braces, now maybe glasses. This is so not happening!"

"It won't be so bad. You'll stand out in the crowd, LOL. Are you going to tell your mom about your eyes?" asks Candice.

"I don't think I'll have to. I think Mrs. Pew is going to call her tonight."

"Yeah, that's tough," says Candice.

{{{DING! DING! DING!}}}

"What's that sound?" says Candice.

"Oh, yeah, it's my cell phone. It's the notification chime from a text message," I say.

"Wow! You have a cell phone?"

"Yup! My mom bought it for emergencies."

"Who is it?" asks Candice leaning over to look.

"It's Calvin. He sent me a picture of the questions from English class."

{{{Ding, Ding, Ding}}}

"Goodness! He sent the same message. I guess somethings never change"

"Calvin sent the same message twice, haha… Heyyyyy, wait a minute, how come he knows about your phone and I don't?"

"Calvin is a tech head. He helped me set it up, LOL."

"Hmm, I'm going to ask if I can have a phone too. We can text each other at night when we're not asleep; that would be so cool, right, Alex?" says, Candice.

"Yeah! You'll tell me secrets and I'll tell your secrets."

"Yeah—no wait, no…" says Candice. "Haha! Funny, Ms. Knowitall."

The ride home is bumpy as usual, and it is hard for me to copy down Candice's sentences. She was nice enough to offer, but I guess I'll copy the ones Calvin sent over in text when I get home and do my homework.

"Hey Candice, Sissy was very quiet today. I'm going to call her later and get the 411." (That's information for those who don't know, LOL.)

"Yeah, you're right." says Candice.

"Oh well, see you later, Alex,"

"Okie dokie, dudette."

I run across the street to my house, and I see my mom's car is in the driveway. I wonder why she's home so early.

Mom is the head nurse at Tallulah Toot County Hospital, that's one county over from Mongolia Groove County, where we live. She loves to help people in their times of need. My mom has been working there since she graduated nursing school ten years ago. She's smart and a lot of fun, and she really knows how to make you feel comfortable. Everyone there loves her.

{{Keys jiggling}}} {{SLAM}}

"Hi Mom," I yell as I rush upstairs to my room.

"Alex, honey, please come here."

"Okay, Mom, I'll be right down after I drop my books in my room."

— CHAPTER FIVE —
SAY IT AIN'T SO, PART 2

When I come back down my mom is waiting for me with a serious look on her face.

Uh oh! What did I do now?

"I received a call from the school today from Mrs. Pew, the English Teacher. She thinks you are having trouble seeing the blackboard in class. Is that true?"

"Well…"

"Please be honest."

"Well…yes. It was the strangest thing, Mom. After I told my friends about me getting braces, we all went into class to take our seats. We were instructed to copy the questions from the blackboard. I wasn't that far back, but I couldn't make out the words; they were blurry.

I did everything to clear them, but nothing worked."

"Well, what about now? Read this passage." Mom held up a letter sitting on the table.

"I can see this fine. I'm having trouble seeing far away."

"Well that my dear is "Near Sighted." I'll make an appointment for you to have your vision checked."

"Oh, Mom, NOT AGAIN."

"I don't know what to tell you, honey. You don't want to look like me?" Mom laughs. She wears glasses too.

"No, I think you look great."

I go upstairs and text Calvin.

"*Hey Calvin, thanks for the sentences for English class.*"

"*Hey, no problem,*" texts Calvin.

"*Hey, no problem,*" texts, Calvin…again!

Wow, you're kidding, right? Calvin repeats himself in a text too, haha. That's my buddy.

"Mom, can I call Sissy for a few minutes?"

"Is your homework done, Ms. Missy?" says Mom.

"No, but I only need a minute."

"Okay, one minute, and I mean one minute."

"Cool, I'll call from the house phone. I don't want to use up my minutes on my cell phone."

The phone just rings and rings. There is no answer. I am getting a little worried. I wait about five minutes and call again.

"Hello, Sillington residence, this is Sissy."

"Hey, dudette, what's up? Are you okay?"

"Oh—Hey, Alex, yeah. My mom put me in gymnastics class. It's hard and tiring," explains Sissy.

"Why did she do that?"

"She says I need to do more physical activities for exercise."

"Wow, dudette, that's rough. Well, we all can use some exercise. 'Exercise…Exercise, come on everybody, do some exercise – now freeze!'" I sing.

"Whatever Alex, I'm beat… I'll see you tomorrow."

"Okay, bye!"

Wow, Sissy sounds so bummed out. Hope she's better tomorrow. I need her silliness. I'm the one that needs cheering up. BRACES AND GLASSES, imagine that!

One day goes by and Mom tells me my appointment for my braces is Saturday.

THAT'S IN FOUR DAYS! Good grief.

But not only that, I am having my eyes checked the same day before I get my braces.

Whoa! Double bubble whammy!

I wonder, if I act like I'm sick, will Mom feel sorry for me and not take me to either of the appointments?

Hmm…nope! Mom is too wily for that, she can out clever me anytime. You can't fool a Knowitall, so that won't work.

I am very nervous about everything. I can't concentrate, all I can think about is Braces and Glasses, Braces and Glasses, Braces and Glasses. It's driving me koo-koo!

I won't let this beat me! I can do this, I can do this, I CAN DO THIS!

Everyone will want to look like me, says the nervous chatter in my head.

Finally, it's Friday. Man, this week went by fast!

Yawning, I get ready for school and gather all

my homework and stuff, and I head downstairs for breakfast.

"Good morning, sweet pea!" says Mom

"Morning," I say.

"Why the long face, honey?"

"Mom, I can't believe you're asking me that. Why me!?!"

"Why not you, Alex? No one is exempt from things they don't want to do. We all grow from our experiences.

Honey, it is only temporary. "

"I know, I know, it's all good".

"Come give Mom a hug. It's going to be fine. Now what about breakfast?"

"No thanks, I'm not hungry. I'll just eat an apple.

Hey! I heard an apple a day keeps the doctors away!"

"Oh Alex, have a nice day!" Mom laughs.

Just then my screwball brother runs down the stairs and yells "No time for breakfast, Mom. I have practice this morning and this afternoon, bye!"

Andrew.

"That boy!" Mom yells.

I walk outside and my BFF Candice is coming out of her house at same time.

"Good Morning, Miss Knowitall!" says Candice.

"Hey!" I say.

"Dang! Is that all I get? What happened to "Hey dudette"? Where's your pep?" Candice pouts.

"I left my *pep* in my room under the covers, I'm still sleepy."

"Alex, you know it's really great that you're trying to be positive about your braces and all. Just think, when it's all said and done, you'll have pretty straight teeth!"

I just look at Candice and shake my head, yes. BFFs are supposed to be there for you when you need them. Candice is a great gal pal.

"Come on, we better hurry before the bus leaves us," Candice says laughing as we run towards the bus stop.

I run behind her laughing too. I stepped up my pep.

"Look at all the kids waiting at the bus stop," I say.

"Yeah, and its 7:30 am on the nose. Our driver is always on time," says Candice.

{{Vroom, Vroom}} 7:40 am, and the bus arrives.

"Look guys, a new driver," one of the kids yells.

"Yeah, and the bus number is different too," another kid shouts back.

The new bus driver is a lady.

— CHAPTER SIX —
HOORAY FOR MS. MATTIE

"Hiya, kids, come aboard! Hope everyone has a great day. This is the beginning of the weekend!" says the lady bus driver.

As the rest of the kids hop on the bus, we all start cheering and chanting: "YAY! It's the end of the week! Hey, Go, Hey! It's the end of the week! Hey, Go, Hey!"

But then I remember, I will be sitting in the eye doctor's office AND the dentist office tomorrow.

"Keep it positive, Alex," I say to myself.

This bus driver is more fun than our last bus driver. He was not a pleasant person.

The bus driver sings bits and pieces from different songs, like: "*The bug's crawl in, the bugs crawl out… in your ears and out your snout.*"

"That's pretty cool," I say laughing.

After she repeats it a few times, all the kids on the bus join in.

Then she sings another song: "*The boys are made out of greasy, grimy, gopher guts, stained grass, and hockey pucks...*"

Now that one *is* funny. I laugh again.

The boys start chanting "boo!" and the girls sing even louder repeating after the bus driver. It is so noisy on the bus, but the new driver makes it fun.

It used to be so dull, and the driver was so unpleasant; we would all just sit there scared to speak.

"Alex, you are so silly, that was not funny," says Candice.

"Oh yeah, if it wasn't funny why did everyone join in?' I say with a smirk.

"Idk," (that's "I don't know" for the uncool kids) says Candice.

We arrive at school a little before 8:00 am, and as we exit the bus, the driver shouts, "Thanks for riding along with Ms. Mattie! I'll see you when you get out of school. I'll be right here, bus 711."

Ms. Mattie, that's her name, is a hoot and a holler, (meaning she's fun).

"Oh great, look who's outside the school?" I say.

"Oh no, Principal Hardhead," says Candice.

"Alright T.K. Spittle Middle students, please proceed to your homeroom classes right away. The bell will ring in approximately four minutes," announces Principal Hardhead.

"Morning Principal Hardhead," I say.

"Morning Principal Hardhead," says Candice.

"And a good morning to you too!" says Principal Hardhead.

As I enter the school everyone is rushing around. You can hear all the lockers slamming closed all at once. Candice and I rush to our lockers and grab our books.

Bell number 1......... {{RING}}

We better hurry. If the second bell rings, we are burnt toast. This middle school thing is the pits!

Me and Candice run so fast, she trips into the classroom and I slide into the class, hitting homeroom base!

Bell number 2.......... {{RING}}

YES! We just make it.

Jeepers Creepers, this is too intense.

I hope no one breaks a kneecap getting to class on time.

"Hey, hey, Alex," says Calvin.

"Hey there, Calvin," I say.

"Are you going, are you going to be able to see, to see the board today, Alex?" asks Calvin.

"Well, let's see, Calvin. Let me ask my eyes that question. Of course, silly willy," I shout.

{{Clap, clap, clap}}

"Good morning, classy. How are y'all this fine day?" says Mrs. Pew, the French-Country-English teacher.

"I hope everyone has their homework assignment. Ten questions copied and answered, oui," she says with a snooty look. (Oh, by the way, oui means yes in French.)

All of a sudden a blaring siren starts sounding.

"Okay classy, please form a double line and partner with someone as we head out into the school yard," says Mrs. Pew.

"What, what's happening? What's happening?" asked Calvin frantically.

"Classy, we are having a practice fire drill, so let's move quickly," says Mrs. Pew.

Wow, Sissy is just getting to school. She's late. I wonder if it's because of the gymnastics class. My poor BFF, she likes to be creative and silly, maybe that stuff isn't for her.

"Hey, Alex, what's going on?" says Sissy.

"We're having a practice run fire drill. I actually think it's kind of cool. We need to know what to do and where to go if there is a real fire in the school. T. K. Spittle is ten times bigger than our old elementary school and we've never had a practice drill."

"Yeah, you're right. We'd better take this seriously and pay attention," says Sissy.

Whoa! You, being serious, Sissy Sillington?

"Alright girls, come along, come along. Stop your chatter. Everyone please be quiet and head out the door marked exit straight ahead of you. When you get outside bear to the right and stand near the basketball court," instructs Mrs. Pew.

"Step aside, coming through, NO TALKING," says Stanley, the nerdy hall monitor.

"Who is this kid?" Sissy says laughing.

"Stanley, he sure takes his hall duties seriously," I say.

"Whoa, it's hot out here, like an Indian summer. I love it. It's going to be a good day, I feel it. I mean we already started off good by leaving class for a fire drill, I wonder what's next."

"Alex, please don't make any wishes for things to happen. Let's just have a normal day," says Candice.

"Yeah Alex, Alex Yeah! I, I don't want any trouble, no trouble for today. I'm looking forward to science class. Professor Kindof said today is the day we dissect a bug!" says Calvin.

"Eww Calvin, you're such a little mad scientist. We girls don't want to dissect anything. And I speak for all girls," I say.

"And I'm not getting anything on my clothes, especially not bug juice," says Candice.

"What's bug juice, Candice?" Sissy asks chuckling.

"It's the stuff that comes out of your mouth when you're laughing, Sissy," I reply.

"Haha! Very funny, Alex," says Sissy.

"Hey, dudette, you asked for it, LOL."

"Nope, nope, nope....Alexandria P. Knowitall, how can you say US girls don't want to dissect anything, when I remember last year you talked about how you couldn't wait to dissect creepy things in science class when we got into middle school?" says Sissy.

"Yeah, well….Whatever dudette. I'm not afraid! Bring it on!"

"Girl, I know you're not scared to get your hands dirty. I know I'm ready. WE'RE with you Calvin!" says Sissy.

— CHAPTER SEVEN —
SWITCH GEARS, THE WEEKEND'S NEAR

Dang! It's been an hour and we are still out here. I'm tired of standing.

I look across from where me and the crew are and I can see about ten girls in our school cheerleading uniform kicking their legs up and chanting, "We are the mighty Timber Wolves" *{{clap-clap, clap-clap}}*. They are cheering loudly and doing all kinds of flips and stuff. I think they are seventh and eighth graders. They look like they know what they're doing.

"Hey! Why do they get to practice during classroom time? I thought all extra curriculum activities take place after school," I say.

"Well, Ms. Knowitall, when there is a home game that day, the cheerleaders and Pom Pom squad get to practice because they will be participating in the game," says Candice.

"And how do you know this, dudette?" I ask.

"My sister is a cheerleader at her high school. I hear all the gossip about what goes on there. I know I shouldn't eavesdrop, but…LOL," explains Candice.

"Hmmm, are you going to try out for the Timber Wolves Squad, Candice?"

"I haven't really thought about it. What about you, Alex?"

"I might, might try out for the, the football team, football team," says Calvin.

Oh my goodness, Calvin shouldn't try out for football. Those guys will knock him into next week and he will probably repeat everything three times instead of two.

"I can see that happening," Sissy laughs.

"Well, I wouldn't mind running," says Sissy, giggling. "I sometimes do it all the way home. Do we have a track team here?"

"Yeah, I think we do. I saw them in the gym doing laps the other day. They were breathing so hard their hearts look like they were leaving their chests." I laugh.

"I think I can handle it, in fact I know I can handle it!" says a determined Sissy.

{{RING-DING-DONG}}
(Announcement)
EVERYONE CAN NOW PROCEED WITH YOUR REGULAR CLASS SCHEDULE.
PLEASE ENTER THE BUILDING QUIETLY!

It's about time they let us back in the school. This was a practice fire drill not a real one.

"What time is it?" I ask.

"Umm, it's 11:15, and it's our lunch break," says Candice.

"I wonder what's for lunch today," says Sissy.

"I saw on the menu, on the menu this morning, hot dogs, but I don't, I don't know what comes with it, with it." says Calvin.

"Hmm, I can go for some franks (those are hot dogs to you)," I say.

"Wow guys look at the line!" says Candice.

"Yeah, I see!" I say. "I think the fire drill messed up our lunch period. All the grades are here and there's only two servers. I'm hungry!"

I tell you this middle school thing is the pits!

"Oh well, I'm going to hip hop on over to the salad bar and get some veggies," says Candice.

"Well, you go right ahead Miss Nola Rabbit, I want my hot dog!" I say.

"Me too," says Sissy.

"Me three, me three," says Calvin.

"Okay, well let's get in there," I say. "On your mark… set… go!"

Calvin, Sissy, and me crash through the crowd. We are yelled at and called names, but we don't care. All we know is, we want hot dogs and we are not going to skip lunch because of the mad rush of all the grades eating at the same time.

"It's kind of cool in middle school that we get to pick what we want and not have to take what they give," Sissy giggles.

By the time we get our lunch, we only have five minutes to eat. I don't see Candice again until the next class.

As Calvin sits down to eat his lunch, he has his lips poking out and pouting.

"Hey, little dude, what's your problem?" I say.

"I really wanted to go to science class today. I was hoping, hoping to dissect a bug. Don't you, don't you think it would be cool to see what's in a bug, what's in a bug, Alex?" says Calvin.

"Umm, No Calvin, but I'll do it if I have to. Smart Alecks keep it smart. Besides, why would

anybody want to see what's in a bug belly. They are so small. They can't have veins and stuff."

"That, that is right, Alex. Insects don't have veins or arteries, but they do, but they do have circulatory systems. Insect blood, also, also called hemolymph. It's a fluid equivalent to blood. It flows, it flows freely through the body cavity and makes direct contact, direct contact with organs and tissues," says Calvin.

I just look at Calvin with one eyebrow up. I know he is smart and all, but dang! I'm so proud of that little dude, but that doesn't change that fact that I'm glad we didn't have to go to science class. I'm not sure I'm ready to do that yet. I know, I know I said I couldn't wait, but a girl has the right change her mind, LOL.

Five, four, three, two—our time is up.

{{ RING}}
LUNCH IS OVER

"Come on guys, that was bell one. We need to hurry before bell two rings," I yell.

Me, Calvin, and Sissy run so fast, Sissy trips into the classroom, Calvin rolls into the room, and I slide into the music class, hitting home base!

I wonder if Sissy has told her mom what we have to do to get to class on time. We are all exercising!

"There's got to be a better way," I say laughing.

Candice is already in the room, hoping she does not have to sing her solo.

Mrs. Clefnote told Candice to learn the song she gave her last week because she was going to have to sing it for class. Well, today is the day!

Hey! No Mrs. Clefnote. There is a note on the board that she is out sick. Lucky for Candice. We have a substitute teacher.

The sub is a large, very well-dressed man with salt and pepper hair, fair skin, and a soft voice.

He reminds me of someone, but I can't think who. He has a great smile and he seems very nice.

"Come in, come in, class. Welcome! As you can see Mrs. Clefnote is out for the day. My name is Mr. Harmony and I will be your substitute teacher. I'm from Sowell, Georgia. I'm married with two grown children, Jason and Janice. I am a retired music teacher from Magnolia University, and I love to record music," says Mr. Harmony.

"How many of you are interested in digital recording?"

A few kids raise their hands.

"Me! Me!" says Jacob.

"Yeah, me!" says Michael.

"Yes, me too!" says, Sissy.

"Would you all like to see a demonstration of a small music production in the works?" asks Mr. Harmony.

The whole class yells at once, "YES!"

The classroom is filled with noise and excitement.

Everyone gathers around the teacher.

"Okay, okay, settle down," says, Mr. Harmony.

He cranks up the classroom computer and pops in a CD.

"Class, this CD has a music production program on it. The program will allow me to create a song," says Mr. Harmony.

When he puts the CD in, it starts making weird noises, and he explains it is loading the program. When it stops loading, the music program pops up on the screen and there are all kinds of gadgets. The class gasps as Mr. Harmony explains the different functions in the music program.

When he finishes explaining, he pushes a button and music starts playing. It is the type of music that makes you want to dance. We all bust a move! Boy, I wish you guys could see Sissy go!

Mr. Harmony shows us how he put it together and it is very simple, but only if you have an ear for music. With one click of a button, he inserts what he calls music loops. The loops make up a lot of different cool sounds.

He even has hip hop music. You know, for a rap song. One by one he pulls up many different sounds and before we know it, he has made a whole song.

Mr. Harmony asks if anyone would like to try it and Sissy literally leaps across the room so fast, those other two guys don't stand a chance.

Sissy concentrates as Mr. Harmony shows her some tricks.

Wow, look at Sissy go, she's making a great song. She's so creative! It takes her no time to get the hang of it. I told you she loves creative things.

Mr. Harmony even records Sissy's song and puts it on a CD for her to take home. Lucky kid!

Those other two boys are mad! They didn't get to participate, and they can't believe how good Sissy is at producing music.

{{RING}}

"Well, class, that's all for today. I hope to see you again. Have a great weekend!" says Mr. Harmony

All my classmates bellow, "Thanks Mr. Harmony!"

"My pleasure, class!" says Mr. Harmony.

CHAPTER EIGHT

MORE CLASS, NOT DONE YET

Candice, Sissy, Calvin, and I talk about music class all the way to gym. We had so much fun. I might want to go get one of those music programs and play around with it. I can sing just a little. Maybe I can become a famous producer!

"Oh Alex, you don't know what you want to be when you grow up. Every time someone says what they are doing, you change your mind and say you want to do that too," says Candice.

"Aww, fish sticks, I do not! I'm just doing what the grown-ups do," I say.

"And what is that?" says Candice.

"I'm weighing my options, LOL."

Me and my pals all walk into the gym at the same time. It's quiet and no one's there. I wonder where everyone is.

"Look, look guys, the sign, the sign there says to report, report to room 148, room 148 – Health," says Calvin.

"Oh no!!! Does this mean we are late for class?" says Sissy.

Room 148 is just around the corner on the same floor as the gym.

We arrive in classroom 148. Mr. Homely is not our Health teacher. I rub my eyes. They are a little blurry, and I walk closer to the board. It says Ms. Weatherburn, but Ms. Weatherburn was not here yet.

My classmates are spread all around the class, talking and laughing. I guess we will have another free period (meaning no class).

After about ten minutes or so, Ms. Weatherburn shows up. She walks in very slowly like she's floating. She is wearing a long black dress with a long black coat to match and I can't see her feet. Her skin is very fair, her lips are pale,

and her hair is blonde with a yellow flower in it. Her eyes are hazel green and she has deep dimples in her cheeks. To me she looks ghost-like.

The teacher glances at the board, then back at us.

"Hello, I am Ms. Weatherburn, and this is Health 148…Welcome.".

Eww, she's very dry. I hope she spices it up a little. She sounds like she's in pain.

"You there, what is your name?"

"Alex."

"No, no, no, your full name?"

"Alexandria P. Knowitall, ma'am".

"Good. And you, what is your name?"

"Candice Smug."

"Ms. Smug and Ms. Knowitall, please pass out the Health books. Once you have received your books, class, we will have a discussion. Today's lesson will focus on hygiene. You there, what is your name?"

"Robert."

"Robert, what?" persists Ms. Weatherburn.

"Robert, what, what?" says Robert, confused.

"Do you have a last name, Robert?"

"Yeah, it's Scott."

"Well then, Mr. Scott, I have a question for you. What is the first thing you do when you get up in the morning?"

"Umm, I run downstairs to eat breakfast," says Robert.

"Class, can someone tell me, is this the right thing to do?"

"No," I say.

"Then what do YOU do, Ms. Knowitall?"

"I get up and take a shower or wash my face."

"Okay, very good."

"What about you, Ms. Smug?"

"I look in the mirror and I say, good morning girlfriend, we are going to have a fabulous day! Then I wash up. I dare not come to the table to eat without washing up. My mom will get on me."

"And how about you? And your name is?"

"Hi, hi, I'm Calvin, Calvin Clueless, ma'am, yes ma'am. I, I run downstairs to, to eat like, like Robert."

Robert and Calvin gave each other a high five. *{{SLAP!}}*

"What was that song the bus driver was singing to us about boys, LOL?" I say.

"Whatever, Alex," says Robert.

"Class, it is very important to pay attention to your personal hygiene. You are all at the age where your body is changing," explains Ms. Weatherburn.

"Good hygiene will keep you healthy. If you pay more attention to yourself, it can help keep you from becoming ill.

"Be sure to wash your hands before you eat and after you have used the bathroom.

"Think about creating a routine for yourself, so you don't forget some of the important stuff."

(The whole class laughs and screams "Eww!")

"Yeah, like using deodorant." I laugh.
"Okay, that's enough, Ms. Knowitall."
"Sorry!"
"Okay, class, our time is almost up. Please read chapter one, "Personal Hygiene". We will discuss more next week."

{{RING}}

"Have a good day and remember, if you stay clean all the time, you don't have to worry about nasty grime, ha..ha..ha!"

{{RING}}

"LOL, I don't know who she's talking to, LOL. The class emptied out on the first bell, LOL. We

69

can't be late. That silly willy teacher! She was kind of scary though, LOL," says Sissy.

"Yeah, I know," agrees Candice.

Candice stops along the way to fix her hair in the reflection of a classroom door.

"Seems a lot of teachers are absent today. Please, please, please, let Ms. Twizzle be here today," says Sissy.

"Yeah, I know, but it's been fun, don't you think, dude and dudettes?" I say.

"That's, that's great Alex, just great! I guess, I guess you're over being nervous, being nervous about your, your braces and maybe glasses," says Calvin.

"Oh shoot yeah, Calvin! Actually, Well, kind of, sort of. I forgot for a second until you brought it up. I'll be the princess of BLING! This is going to be an interesting year, especially if I need glasses too," I say sarcastically.

"We said, we said, over and over, you'll be fine," says Calvin.

"I'm so happy you're being a trooper about this, you will be pretty when it's all over," says Candice.

"Yeah, there's no need to get all worked up. It is what it is, right?"

"Yup"

I look at Candice and I start to get a little testy, but I can't. She's right. When it's all over, I'll look great.

How can I get mad at my BFF? So, I put on my big girl pants and I go on with my day.

— CHAPTER NINE —
ALL FIZZLED OUT

I rush into Art scared of being late. Ms. Twizzle is sitting in the back of the room on the windowsill swinging her legs while she watches us come in. Any minute, she will be twisting around the room like a kite.

I guess the incident with the window didn't scare her.

"Hi, class! Are you ready to draw your way into a magical castle? Let's see who the real artists are in this class. No pressure, just fun!" says Ms. Twizzle.

"Alex, dear, why the long face?"

"I was just reminded of an eventful day I will have tomorrow," I say.

"Oh wow, groovy, that's a good thing, right? It's okay to talk to Ms. Twizzle," she says.

"Tomorrow I am getting braces on my teeth," I say.

"Oh, is that all? When I was a kid I had braces too! At first I was embarrassed, but as time passed, I got used to it.

"My teeth looked like they were running away from my mouth, LOL. Instead of being mad and sad about it, I joked about it along with my classmates. I joked about it so much the other kids wondered why I did it. What they didn't realize was, I was beating them in their own game. They started feeling bad and stopped teasing me, but I doubt if you will have the same problem. The kids here think you're great," says Ms. Twizzle.

"Wow, Thanks, Ms. Twizzle," I say.

"Alex dear, you will be okay. Kids like your personality and your Smart Alecky remarks. In a silly kind of way they look up to you. I doubt if the braces will take that away from you," she says. "Are you okay now?"

"Yup!" I say.

"OKAY! NOW, DRAW ME THAT CASTLE!"
she says as she twirls around in a circle.

And just like that, Ms. Twizzle skates off to the
front of the classroom.

After talking to Ms. Twizzle and my BFFs, I
realize this may not be so bad, LOL.

I don't like to be negative, so again, I'm pulling
up my big girl pants.

Negativity has no class; it's not a part of my curriculum, LOL.

"When everyone has finished, please bring your drawings to the front of the class. I would like to put them on the board for everyone to see," says Ms. Twizzle.

Ms. Twizzle examines all the pictures on the board one by one. She is really impressed with all the drawings. She never says a bad word about anyone's pictures. Ms. Twizzle loves art and she feels everything around her is a connection to art.

"Aww, yes….Oh! My, my, my….very good! This one here is very dramatic. I love it, I love it! Haha. You darlings have captured the mystical essence of medieval times. I must display this outside my room, yes, yes, I must," says Ms. Twizzle.

I start having issues with my sight again. It is a little hard for me to see. I stare at one of the pictures so hard I swear the horse in the picture is moving.

My eyes are playing tricks on me. Oh goodness, what is happening to me? In the last two periods, my eyes were fine!

But, we weren't reading anything and everything I looked at was close to me. Mom said

I MIGHT be near sighted. I can't be. I'm a 20/20 vision kind a gal, haha.

Many of my classmates crowd around the front of the room to see each other's pictures. I stand in the back. I can't see that far, plus I am short. I'm only 4 feet 11 inches.

"Alex dear, why are you squinting? Can you see, my child?" says Ms. Twizzle.

"Not really," I mumble.

"Dear, dear come here," says Ms. Twizzle.

"Maybe you need your eyes checked. Have you discussed this with your parents?"

"Yeah, yeah, I know. This is my other Saturday morning treat. My mom scheduled an appointment for me tomorrow," I explain.

"Good girl! I want you to be able to see the wonderful world of COLOR!"

And once again, just like that, she skates off to another part of the room.

You know, sometimes I think Ms. Twizzle is not a real person, haha.

I really like art class; you know how I know?

It goes by really fast. Before I know it, it's time

to go. We do so many fun things, I don't keep track of time.

"Alright class, I would like to recruit a few of you to help tape some of your pictures outside the room on the bulletin board," says Ms. Twizzle.

Calvin, Candice, Michael, and Alexis will you be my little helpers?

"Yes, yes, ma'am," says Calvin.

"Far out! Right-on! Groovy! I want to get these up before the bell rings. The rest of you, start cleaning your areas. You dig! Thank you!"

"Hey Alex, do you want to come over to my house later? You can help me curl my hair?" says Candice.

"Sure. I'll have to ask my mom," I say.

"It's the weekend! And besides you need to take your mind off tomorrow. Let's have some fun, dudette. My sister is having a few friends over this evening. Let's see what they talk about, LOL," says Candice.

{{RING}}

"Alright class, I'll catch you on the flip side!"

"Where does Ms. Twizzle get her sayings, I love her personality," says Sissy.

DING – DONG – DING
ANNOUNCEMENTS
Good afternoon, students, next week will kick-off T.K. Spittle Middle's Super Duper Candy Fundraiser. Win great prizes! Fundraiser packets will be handed out in homeroom on Monday, so don't forget to get yours! Tell your friends and tell your family. SELL, SELL, SELL!
Have a super weekend!
DING – DONG – DING

— CHAPTER TEN —
IN MY COMFORT ZONE

"That'll be fun," I say.

"What??" says Candice.

"Selling candy! Remember how we used to have to walk around the neighborhood with our parents to sell candy for elementary school? Well, now we can do it ourselves! We're in middle school now. They can't treat us like babies."

"Oh, yeah…I remember. Do my pants look right, they feel twisted?" asks Candice.

"Hey, dudette, I'm not looking down there. People will think I'm weird," I say. "Hey, look over there…It's Ms. Mannie."

"No, Alex, It's Ms. Mattie," corrects Candice.

"Oh yeah, right, Ms. Mattie," I agree.

Ms. Mattie is standing in front of our lucky bus number 711, and she's summoning all her kids to get on the bus.

Ms. Mattie is very punctual. She wants to get everyone home quickly, I guess so she can get her weekend started. Me, I'm thinking Braces and Glasses, Braces and Glasses.

Tomorrow is THE DAY! Think positive, Alex. Think positive, I say to myself.

The kids join in with Ms. Mattie, singing and telling jokes all the way home. Even Candice joins in this time.

I sit quietly, imagine that. All the way home I think about what I will look like with braces and glasses, and from my perspective the picture looks a little funny, haha.

"See ya, Alex, I'll call you!" says Candice.

Mom's not home this time when I arrive. I put my key in the lock and open the door to complete silence. I've gotten so use to coming home to Mom here cooking or doing yard work. I lock the door behind me (can't be too careful these days) and go to the kitchen to make myself a PB & J sandwich (I

know you know what a PB & J is) and some milk, one of my favorite combinations, and I watch an episode of a cartoon about a family who live in the stone age.

This is an old cartoon from the 60s and 70s that my mom used to watch when she was a kid.

She's still a kid at heart. Mom bought a streaming channel with all the old cartoons she grew up on and watches them every Saturday morning as if the times haven't changed. I know you're probably tired of me saying it, but my mom is so much fun!

Should I do my homework now or wait until Sunday? I think to myself.

Aww, let's just get it over with so I can have the weekend to myself. I have got to focus on making my mark in T.K. Spittle Middle School and not on the "Braces and Glasses".

"Nobody knows the trouble I've seen. Nobody knows the sorrow," I sing out loud and rock back and forth on the couch, LOL. I crack me up.

{{The door slams}}

"Mom, is that you. Boy, am I glad your home!"

"No dingy, it's not mom," says my goofy brother, Andrew.

Oooh! He makes me so mad!

{{The door slams, Again}}

"Mom, you're home! Boy, am I glad to see you."

"Hi honey, are you alright? You look like you have things on your mind."

"Boy, do I, but I'm better now that you're home, Mom."

"Hey there Andrew, how was your day" says Mom.

"Hey mom, it was a good day. I hit two three pointers today at practice," says Andrew.

"Hey! That's my son," says Mom.

"Thanks, Mom," says Andrew, then he turns to me and makes a face.

After Mom's meddled around for a while, she cooks dinner, and we sit down to eat. I know, I know, I just had a PB&J sandwich. What can I say? I'm a growing kid! Haha.

Conversations at the dinner table are interesting to say the least.

"So Alex, how was your day?" Mom asks.

"Well, Mom, my day was a lot of fun, until Calvin brought up the braces and glasses thing. That made the end of my day a little yucky! But you know me, Mom, I keep it positive and I pop back into place," I say.

"Alex, dear, there is no need to worry. Change is a part of life and life is a part of change, so, honey, roll with it. I know when it's all said and done, you will look

fabulous!" Mom said laughing.

Mom and I start singing together, "Rollin, rollin, rollin… rollin, keep it rollin," Haha!

Mom and I laugh and laugh. She knows how to make me

feel better.

Andrew just sits there and says nothing. I think he feels a little sorry for me. Any other time he would be cracking jokes.

I pop some popcorn and Mom takes some juice out of the refrigerator, and we sit and watch a funny movie called "My Clumsy Mailman."

I think they made this movie about our mailman. He is always falling over and stepping on my Mom's beautiful flowers.

Andrew goes to his room to play video games.

{{Yawn and stretch}}

"Mom, I think I'll go to bed now," I say.

"Okay dear, you have a big day tomorrow. I'll see you in the morning," says Mom.

"Okay, good night!" I say.

Mom stays downstairs and continues to watch TV. She's a night owl, whoody who! Haha.

Remember today we talked about hygiene?

I've gotta go and shower and prepare for bed.

{{Clearing my throat}}

"Me, me, me, me, me, me, me…Me, I gotta be me. Who else could I be? I gotta be me!"

"Shut your face, brat!" says Andrew.

"Whatever, butt-breath!" I yell back.

My *slightly* older brother, Andrew is thirteen and in the 8th grade and yes, he also goes to T.K. Spittle Middle school. They should have lost his entrance paperwork. He is so not cool. THANK GOODNESS, I don't see him in school often. He plays basketball and practices a lot. And this is his last year before he goes to High School. And you know what I say……BYE!

Even though he can be annoying, I love my brother and I know secretly he loves me too.

— CHAPTER ELEVEN —
STRANGE HAPPENING

It's Saturday morning. Mom wakes me up. I jump out of bed. I am too nervous to eat, so I don't. I wash and dress myself and I'm ready to go. I guess Mom does the same.

I jump in Mom's not so perfect car and we head to the eye doctor.

"This ride seems so familiar," I say.

"Alex, let's not start. It's too early for you to panic," Mom says.

"Mom! I'm just saying."

Hmm, same lights, same cars, Ekk! SAME BUILDING!

I'm confused. I've seen all of this before.

Mom and I walk into a big white office building that looks like a block made of Legos. There are lights across the ceiling that look like vines in the jungle and a doorman who opens the door for us and everything. It's so strange.

Coming into the front door to my left there is a snack bar with sandwiches, pastries, fruit, candy, chips, and drinks, like coffee, tea and juice….all the things I like.

"Can I have an apple juice, please?" I ask.

"Hmm, ok, that can't hurt, one small apple juice please," says Mom.

"Thanks Mom, this will help with the butterflies in my stomach. I want to drown these little annoying things."

Mom looks at me confused, but amused at the same time.

"Oookay, you do that," says Mom.

As I walk beside Mom, I spot a huge foot in my path, so big I have to walk around it. I pass it and then look back…then up. There is a huge dinosaur in the middle of the lobby floor.

"Umm, why is that here? It looks like it belongs in a pre-historic museum or something," I ask.

The whole set-up in this building is weird, it's almost like we are in an amusement park.

There are vending machines with medical items in them, like...

Wait! Did that dinosaur move?!?

This thing has gotta be sixty feet tall, but why is it smack dead in the middle of the floor?

Whoa, it did move. I see a kid push an orange button and that thing moves, then another kid pushes a blue button and it roars. It's scaring me silly!

I think it's weird, but everyone seems to be enjoying it.

Mom has no clue what floor we need to go to, so she walks over to a sign that lists all the doctors in the building to see what floor the eye doctor is on. I wonder if she knows his or her name.

I turn around and see something else bizarre. The elevator doors look creepy. They look like the same elevator doors from an amusement park in Florida, you know where the creepy guy takes you for a ride up and down and the elevator drops. Oh, please don't let this be the same.

The elevators are brown, rickety, rusty steel. They are oddly shaped, almost like an eyeball. The numbers over top of the elevator looks like they're part of a dial of some sort.

Mom presses the button to the elevator and "screech, boom!" The doors open like an eye. It looks like someone is just waking up from a deep sleep. The inside of the elevator is pitch black, like our pupils.

There is a person that works in the elevator pressing the buttons for everyone. This person wears black too, so it's hard to see them standing in the elevator. The only thing I can see is their white neck-tie. It looks like it's floating in thin air.

"Hello? Are you there?" I ask.

"Good day, madam, what floor?" says the voice in the dark.

This is spooky, like something straight out of a movie.

I watch Mom as she extends her hand out to push one of the buttons. Strange this time the operator does not stop her.

"Mom! No! What are you doing?"

"Alex! What did I tell you about startling me like that? The eye doctor is on the twelfth floor," Mom says.

"Oh, I thought you were going to press thirteen, haha."

"No silly!"

{{Ding}}

The doors open and all the lights come on. I finally see the tall gentleman, who is operating the elevator. What seems to be a nightmare is over.

"Twelfth floor, watch your step," says the gentleman elevator operator.

We step out of the elevator straight onto a platform. I know, weird, right? And guess what happens, a small boat appears. Was it my imagination or are we in Poomba Boomba Land? The small boat sails in on a narrow Nile of grape soda in the hallway past several rooms.

How do I know it is grape soda? Some splashes on my face and I lick it.

"So which one is the ophthalmologist office?" (That's the eye doctor to you and me, haha.)

Mom and I sail down a long hallway. Each door has the name of a doctor on it.

"Alex honey, do you remember what room we are supposed to go to? I only remembered the floor." Mom says grinning.

Mom doesn't seem to think all this is strange. She acts like this is normal.

"Sure, It's room 1212," I blurt out.

A double blessing.

I'll let you in on a little secret.

My mom's birthday is December 12th and the time of my birth is 12:12am. How cool is that!

The little boat knows exactly where to go and we stop.

Mom and I exit the boat in front of a bright orange door. It's room 1212. The name tag on the door reads, Dr. Theodore Speeks.

"Mom, doesn't the eye doctor's door look like the dentist office's door?"

"Oh Alex, don't be silly, dear. Come on, let's go in."

WHY ISN'T SHE LISTENING TO ME, I yell (to myself, LOL).

Mom and I walk into the eye doctor's office, I feel like a million eyes are watching me. There are racks and racks of eyeglasses all over the place. There are oval-shaped, round-shaped, and even star-shaped glasses. And get this: they are some in a vending machine where you have options. You get to pick the eyeglass frames and colors.

The eye doctor's office is different from the dentist office. Mom just walks up to the front desk to tell the receptionist we are here.

"Yes, I am here, Alexandria P. Knowitall!"

"Insurance card and I.D.," says the receptionist.

Boy! He's a piece of dry ice. I step back and let Mom do her thing.

"Sure, one second," says Mom.

"Alex dear, take, ah, I mean, sit in that chair over there."

"Okie dokie, Smokey."

Mom hands the insurance card and her I.D. to the receptionist, and he gives her four sheets of paper to complete. I guess that's what is done for new patients. Wow! There must be a million questions on that.

Mom and I sit in the waiting area for almost thirty minutes while she completes the paperwork.

"Alexandria," says the eye doctor's assistant.

"Yes," I say.

"Please, follow me."

Finally! I was getting tired of waiting.

I follow the assistant into a dark room. She tells me to sit on a little bar stool and presses my head against a metal bar with clear protective paper on it.

"Now sweetheart, lean forward and open your eyes wide and focus on the little yellow house you see in front of you on the screen. You will feel a puff of air in your eyes; this will test the pressure in your eyes," instructs the eye doctors' assistant.

I'm scared. I don't know what to expect. I sit there and out of nowhere a big puff of air grabs my eye ball. I jump back and close my eyes.

Whoa! That was weird.

"Alexandria sweetheart, you are not supposed to move. I know it's a bit of a shock, but I need to get a reading," says the eye doctors' assistant.

This time I brace myself. I am ready, or so I think. The blast of air comes out again and I jump back, again.

"Are we going to be here all day doing this?" I ask.

"No sweetheart, I was able to get a good reading this time. Oh, by the way, my name is Haiti." says the assistant.

"Let's go take you to the examination room. I have a couple more things to do and then you will see Dr. Speeks."

"Where's my Mom?" I ask.

"Oh, don't worry, she is completing the paperwork. She'll be back here soon."

Dang, she's still doing that?

Haiti instructs me to sit in the black chair and put my head back. SHE IS PUTTING EYE DROPS IN MY EYES!! NO!!

Everything starts looking blurry, just like when I'm in class trying to read the board.

"Alexandria, sit back and close your eyes, and here's a tissue to wipe the access drainage. Dr. Speeks will be in to see you shortly," she says.

I almost fall asleep then Mom walks in.

"Alex honey, are you okay?"

"That lady put eye drops in my eyes, and now my vision is blurry."

"Oh, you mean she dilated your pupils. (That means your pupils were widened so a full examination can be done to check the health of the optic nerve and retina)."

"Yeah, that, what you said."

{{Knock, knock, knock}}

"Good Morning, my name is Dr. Speeks."

"Hi Dr. Speeks, I'm Mrs. Knowitall, Alex's mother."

"Well hello, nice to meet you. Hello Alex or do you prefer Alexandria?"

"Alex, sir," I say.

"Well, okay Alex. I am going to examine your eyes.

Take this black spoon and cover your right eye and sit up straight, now read each line."

"Okay: E, FB,TQZ, LBED, BECFD, EDFCZB"

"Hmm, not quite correct, it should read: E, FP,TOZ, LPED, PECFD, EDFCZP."

"Now, let's try the left eye, same thing."

"Okay: E, FP,TQZ, LBED, PACFD, EDFCZP."

Well not too bad, but you missed a few! As I see it Alex, you will need glasses. In my opinion you are having some difficulty seeing far.

"Mrs. Knowitall, you and Alex can wait in the lobby while I submit Alex's prescription. Today's technology means you won't have to wait long. Also Alex, you can pick your own frames from the cool colorful vending machine in the waiting area ," says Dr. Speeks.

"All man! Great!" I say.

"Why don't you go try some on and bring me the ones you like best," says Dr. Speeks.

"Come Alex, let's go look….fun, right!" says Mom. NOT!

Me and Mom go to the waiting area and pick out three pairs that we think look cool and I try them on.

"Here, I like the round ones," I say looking away.

"Yes, these are cute"

I walk to the back of the office to give the frames I picked out to Dr. Speeks. He tells me to wait in the seating area and I will have my glasses in no time.

"Oh, gee…I can hardly wait," I say *nonchalantly*. (I know, I know…Look it up)

Dr. Speeks walks out and hands me my new glasses.

"Here, put these on," says Dr. Speeks.

"Cool, thanks Doc," I say sarcastically.

Whoa, these things look weird.

"Haha, yes, but you will get use to them in no time," says Dr. Speeks.

"Have a great day you two!"

SMH, glad that's over! (SMH is shaking my head for you dudes and dudettes who don't know.)

"Aww, don't my baby girl look cute!" says Mom.

MOM!

"Hungry, Alex?" Mom asks.

"Boy! Am I."

— CHAPTER TWELVE —
LIFE IS BUT A DREAM

I can't believe I wear glasses now, oh well....

"Alright dear, let's go. One down and one to go. Moving on!" says Mom.

"Yup, yup, moving on!" I say.

Mom suggests we stop to have lunch before my dental appointment. We have an hour to spare.

We stop at the café on the first floor. I want to have one good meal before my teeth scream from the pain. Yes, pain!

My friend Holly from my third period class has braces too. Holly told me once a month I will have to get my braces tightened. Boy! She said it hurts like heck! Solid food is not an option when they are tightened, soup will be my best friend.

Yuck! I don't like soup. Maybe Mom will let me have ice cream. I love ice cream.

Mom and I sit in a nice cozy spot. It looks like a rainforest filled with trees, animals, and stuff. There's even lightning with a sprinkle of rain; its fake though, LOL.

"This is so cool. I love it here," I say.

"Umm hmm, it's pretty neat!" Mom agrees.

I'll have a lava burger, no cheese please, haha, and Mom has the chicken Jungle-Jem salad, eww!

I'm feeling kind of okay about my new journey. Mom assures me I will be fine and I believe her. Most kids may not want to have braces, but I'll embrace it –get it, embrace it, haha. But seriously, I want to be the voice of reason to help them through it. So if you guys out there wanna talk, I'M HERE!

My mom is my best friend. She always supports me. She's a sweet person. Everybody likes her, except for my dad. He left us when I was two and a half years old, but Mom makes sure we are okie dokie.

"Alex honey, we have to hurry. Your appointment is in fifteen minutes," says Mom.

"Okay, Mom, I have one bite left," I say.

I brush the breadcrumbs from the hamburger bun off my shirt, pants, and hands and Mom tips the waiter.

I might want to be a waiter someday, LOL. Waiters make a lot of money in tips, if you have a great personality.

We go back to those weird green and gold elevators on the opposite side of the building, with the person driving them.

Again, I am back on the thirteenth floor.

I really don't like that number. The dental office is in room 1313 and the eye doctor is on the twelfth floor in room 1212. For some reason the two office visits feel strange. It's like the good is battling the evil.

I peek my head through the dental office door and the game station, TV, and everything is there like I remember it.

"Hi, Mrs. Knowitall. Hi, Alex, are you ready to get your braces?" Sadie, the Dental Hygienist greets us.

"Yeah, I'm ready. Let's do this!" I reply.

"Alight Alex, that's the spirit," says Sadie.

"This will be easy. I want you to relax."

Just like any normal kid, I roll my eyes to the back of my head. Can you guys do that, haha?

I'm being nice and practicing my positivity, but I really want this to be over.

Sadie takes me in the back. I hop up on the big dental chair and she leans me back.

Sadie opens my mouth to check certain areas of my mouth. She is mumbling and talking to herself, some of the things she is saying, I don't remember happening.

This is really strange. I must be dreaming.

"Hmm, your teeth and gums look fine, the extractions healed well," says Sadie.

I just look at Sadie and I want to ask, what are you talking about, but I just play along.

Right then Mom walks in and announces she has finished more paperwork, (Financial stuff, I think).

Shortly afterwards, Dr. Giggles walks in. I can smell him before he enters the room.

"Well, well, well, Alexandria P. Knowitall, how are you today?"

"Hi, Dr. Giggles. I'm doing okay. How long will

this take? Is it going to hurt? How long will I have to wear these things?" I ask.

"Hey, hey, slow down, Alex. To answer your questions, I should be done with you in a couple of hours. When I tighten the wires on the braces you will feel some discomfort for a few hours. And, you will need to wear them for eighteen months, depending on your progress."

"Ahh Man! Okay, can we get this over with?" I say.

"Alex, do you want me to stay back here with you?" asks Mom.

"Nah, I'm ok." I want to show Mom I'm a big girl.

"All righty then, I'll be in the lobby reading a magazine. This is exciting!"

"You think so? You wanna trade places, haha. I'm so funny."

"Yes, yes, it's a new adventure, dear, and you and I love adventure!"

"YUP!" I agree. In the back of my mind, I'm saying not all the time.

"Okay, ladies, I want to get started on Alex's mouth." Dr. Giggles laughs.

It's time and I'm so nervous. Dr. Giggles leans my chair back and puts a plastic mouthpiece in my mouth to hold it open. He puts some white stuff on a plate and dips a cloth in it, then rubs it on my teeth.

"What is this for?" I mumble, spitting stuff all over the place.

"It is polishing paste. It will help clean your teeth. Your teeth have to be very clean for me to apply the brackets to stick firmly. Now, shhhh! No talking," says Dr. Giggles.

"Eww, this stuff is nasty!" I say spitting again.

My mouth is open so wide, I could catch flies. My teeth are exposed like a baby's naked bottom. Dr. Giggles says my teeth need to dry. My eyes go wide as I see a jar on the table in front of me with all types of dental tools and another jar labeled bonding cement.

Oh Great! Not only will I have train tracks running through my mouth, there will be a sidewalk to match, LOL!

Dr. Giggles mixes the bonding cement with other stuff then he pulls out a drawer of brackets of all different sizes and colors.

"What color brackets would you like, Alex?"

"Umm, clear," I say.

He says my teeth are average size and the number five brackets should fit nicely. One by one he picks out number five brackets with small tweezers and smears the bonding concrete, I mean cement, on the brackets and affixes each of them to my teeth individually. This is taking too long. I want to see what I look like.

An hour and a half goes by and he's finally finished.

Dr. Giggles cleans up the mess and instructs me to sit for an extra hour.

Sadie comes in with what looks like a glue gun, but it isn't, it's some kind of doohickey with a blue light.

"What is that for?" I ask.

"The blue light from this device is called a dental curing light. It's used on teeth to set the cement," explains Sadie.

"Oh great! A disco in my mouth, LOL!"

"Oh Alex." Sadie laughs.

Sadie shines the blue light on each tooth to set the bond. I am so tired of my mouth being open so wide. There is a tube in my mouth catching all my saliva (that's spit in kid talk, haha). I feel like my tonsils are hanging in the wind.

Sadie can see I'm uncomfortable, so she pulls the mouth guard out.

"Phew! That's better," I say.

An hour goes by. I've almost fallen asleep, but a fowl stench floats by my nose waking me up. Dr. Giggles must be near.

The dentist walks in with several little containers with assorted colored rubber bands and small pieces of wire.

"Alex dear, what color wires would you like to have?" says Dr. Giggles.

"Ah, hmm. I like yellow," I say pointing.

"Yellow it is. Does that go for the rubber bands too?" asks Dr. Giggles.

"Yes, please." I say.

One by one he weaves the wires in and out of each bracket. He scrapes his knuckle on one of them. "Wow! Those must be sharp," I say.

"Well Alex, since you mentioned it, I'm going to give you some dental wax to put on the areas that are sharp to keep you from cutting your cheeks," says Dr. Giggles.

"Train tracks, sidewalk, and chainsaw—what a combination!"

"I'm sure you saw the vending machines with the rubber bands in them, right?"

"Yeah, I did. I think that is so cool. There are tons of cool colors."

Yes there are, so anytime you need new ones, you can come to the office and take some out of the machine, for FREE!

I slide down the chair to leave and Dr. Giggles says, "Where are you going, young lady? I am not done yet."

"WHAT!!! You're kidding me," I say.

"I still need to attach the rubber bands. You did say yellow, correct?"

"Umm hmm," I mutter.

"Knock-Knock, I've come to see the progress," says Mom.

"Oh, yes, yes, come in Mrs. Knowitall. I am just about done with Alex," says Dr. Giggles.

"Aww, Alex, don't you look adorable. Honey,

you don't look bad at all," says Mom.

Without saying a word, I looked at my Mom with a pitiful puppy dog face.

I want to see what I look like, but I'm afraid to see what I look like.

Once again, I'm back in the saddle. I don't need to lean back this time. Dr. Giggles takes a tool that looks like a crochet needle and hooked the bands to the brackets to hold the wire in place.

"All done!" Dr. Giggles takes a deep breath. "Oops! One other thing."

Now he's coming at me with narrow pliers.

"I need to tighten the wires in the braces, you will feel discomfort later. If you feel a stick in your cheek, be sure to put some wax on it. Mrs. Knowitall, please give Alex Tylenol if she starts to feel pain."

"Will do, Dr. Giggles."

"Once a month Alex will need to come in and have her braces tightened. I will continue to supply her with dental wax to help with any discomfort in her mouth. Remember to brush your teeth regularly, Alex and floss to loosen food from the braces," says Dr. Giggles.

"Thank you, doctor," says Mom.

"My pleasure, Mrs. Knowitall," says Dr. Giggles, chuckling.

Mom makes next month's appointment before we leave. As we are walking out the door, I hear someone call my name.

"Alexxx, oh Alexxx, Alexxx, oh Alexxx, We're not done with you yet. Come back, come back, come back!"

I look back and there are creepy doctors and their assistants coming after me with dental tools. I turn around to warn Mom and there she is, standing there with dental tools and a creepy smile on her face too.

{{SCREAM—SCREAM—SCREAM}}

No, no….I toss and turn…No, no!

My mom runs down the hall and bursts into my room.

"Alex, Alex, honey wake up, wake up – you're dreaming."

My arms and legs are flailing all over the place as I wake up.

I open my eyes, sit up and jump back when I see Mom.

I jumped out of my bed and immediately run to the bathroom. I looked in the mirror and they were not there!

I do not have braces and there are no signs of glasses!

I look all around trying to make sense of what just happened.

Just then I realize it was all a dream!!

Gee, that was a trip, but I know eventually soon I'm gonna need braces and glasses. Oh well, I'll be ready, haha.

{{RING}}

"Top of the mornin to ya, Knowitall residence!" I say.

"Hey Alex, what's up?" says Candice.

"Boy, Candice! Have I got a story for you…?"

"Ooo, juicy good stuff, I hope"

"Yup, wait until you hear. We're going to need a vacation after this."

"Well, you know, spring break is around the corner."

"What! Wait! Hold on".

"What?" says Candice.

"I'm going to look around the corner …"

"ALEX!" says Candice.

"Just kidding, dudette. I can't wait, haha!"

THE END!

AUTHOR BIO

Taunya T. D. Said has the ability to keep you bent over in laughter. Still a kid at heart, she can overwhelm you with her daily antics. Now Taunya is ready to share her contagious sense of humor with you.

Taunya resides in Northern Maryland with one daughter, who inspires her journey, her special someone of 22 years, who supports her ambition and their precious Silky Yorkshire Terrier.

AVAILABLE TITLES

Changing Schools and Classroom Rules

Braces AND Glasses, Imagine That!

UPCOMING TITLES

The Vacation From...
Hello Operator, HELP!

Cheerleading Into Some Mess.

The Acting Bug That Bit Me, Youch!

The End of School, Testing... One, Two

SMART ALEC ALEX
ACTIVITY

BRACES AND GLASSES

```
R  E  T  N  E  C  L  A  C  I  D  E  M  R  E  S  V
C  D  J  S  K  E  E  P  S  R  D  A  U  E  O  E  I
D  I  A  S  D  T  M  N  A  L  O  L  Y  L  L  S  S
E  U  X  C  H  E  E  R  L  E  A  D  E  R  S  S  I
Q  L  X  E  S  D  J  C  A  N  D  I  C  E  G  A  O
P  G  H  C  H  A  P  T  E  R  B  O  O  K  E  L  N
L  J  M  G  T  K  S  P  I  T  T  L  E  Z  O  G  Y
W  F  Q  R  Z  M  M  E  T  M  P  H  I  I  R  D  Z
E  E  D  U  D  U  U  Z  L  Q  U  Y  F  P  G  N  H
R  F  G  Y  S  S  I  S  A  G  D  E  S  U  I  A  I
D  Q  I  V  K  M  B  Y  I  R  G  S  S  X  A  S  L
N  D  U  D  E  T  T  E  Q  C  F  I  M  U  R  E  A
A  C  A  L  V  I  N  C  E  F  C  Q  G  V  M  C  R
L  F  T  O  Y  H  U  A  B  A  U  L  O  R  R  A  I
B  J  N  F  I  R  E  D  R  I  L  L  A  O  D  R  O
U  X  E  L  A  C  E  L  A  T  R  A  M  S  I  B  U
O  L  L  A  T  I  W  O  N  K  Z  G  L  T  S  Y  S
```

Andrew	Dude	Museum
BFF	Dudette	Music Class
Braces and Glasses	Fire Drill	Chapter Book
Calvin	Georgia	Sissy
Candice	Hilarious	Smart Alec Alex
Cheerleaders	Know-It-All	T.K. Spittle
Dr. Giggles	LOL	T.D. Said
Dr. Speeks	Medical Center	Vision

SMART ALEC ALEX
WHO'S WHO

1. What is this book about?
2. What are the main characters names?
3. What school do the kids go to?
4. Who is Smart Alec Alex favorite pal?
5. Which character is very nervous and repeats everything twice?
6. Which character worries about their appearance?
7. Which character is very silly ?
8. Can you name any of the teachers in the school?
9. Which character has an annoying brother?
10. Who is your favorite character?